The KITTEN STARS

Kitty Tubers

THE KITTYTUBERS,
Book 2

by Darcy Pattison

Pictures by Nicole Standard

MIMS HOUSE
LITTLE ROCK, AR

For Haileigh, Bruce, Zeke, Gabe, Ash & Neona—
May you find your perfect roles in life!

Mims House
1309 Broadway
Little Rock, AR 72202
mimshouse.com

Publisher's Cataloging-in-Publication Data

Names: Pattison, Darcy, author. | Standard, Nicole, illustrator.
Title: The kitten stars / by Darcy Pattison ; illustrations by Nicole Standard.

Series: The Kittytubers

Description: Little Rock, AR: Mims House, 2021.

Summary: The continuing story of Angel Persian and the kittens of Kittywood. These KittyTubers develop their skills in hopes of being chosen as KittyTube stars.

Identifiers: ISBN: 978-1-62944-169-6 (Hardcover) | 978-1-62944-170-2 (pbk.) |978-1-62944-171-9 (ebook) | 978-1-62944-172-6 (audio) | LCCN 2020916121

Subjects: LCSH Cats--Juvenile fiction. | Internet videos--Juvenile fiction. | Online social networks--Juvenile fiction. | Family--Juvenile fiction. | BISAC JUVENILE FICTION / Performing Arts / Film | JUVENILE FICTION / Readers / Chapter Books

Classification: LCC PZ7.P27816 Ki 2020 | DDC [Fic]--dc23

Contents

— ⭐ —

"… there was something in me at a young age that was not worried about success but was worried about becoming a better actor."

Paul Dano

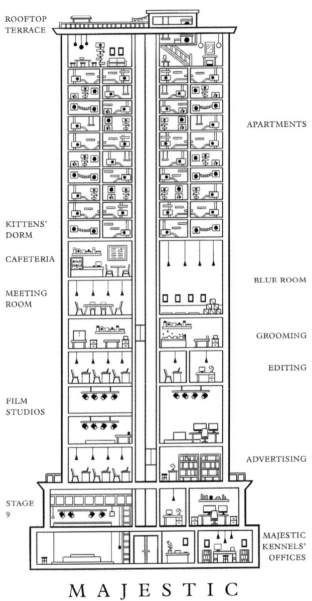

ROOFTOP
TERRACE

APARTMENTS

KITTENS'
DORM

CAFETERIA

BLUE ROOM

MEETING
ROOM

GROOMING

EDITING

FILM
STUDIOS

ADVERTISING

STAGE
9

MAJESTIC
KENNELS'
OFFICES

MAJESTIC
KENNELS

Flipping the Bully

What is a kitten to do when a bully cat steals his catnip?

No fears! No tears!

Underdog Cat will save the day.

She arches her spine and hisses. "Give it back," she says. "Now!"

The bully cat looms over Underdog Cat. The bully cat unsheathes her claws and lashes out.

Underdog Cat dances away without a scratch. She ducks under the bully's outstretched paw and heaves upward. The bully flips upside down.

"Ow!" the bully cries. She stares at Underdog Cat and shakes her head. She turns tail and runs.

As the kitten nibbles his catnip, he looks up at Underdog Cat with adoring eyes.

Underdog Cat saves the day!

Again.

The KittyTubers

JUST KITTEN AROUND Joke

Q: Why are kittens so good at video games?

A: Because they have nine lives.

Views. Angel Persian's life was ruled by views. If humans ignored her videos, life was terrible. But when they watched her, liked her, and shared her, life was amazing. Glorious. Wonderful.

Angel dashed up the last few steps and crashed through the double doors into the dorm hallway. She could've taken the elevator up to the tenth floor, but she'd been too excited to wait for it at this time of day. Just before dinner, the elevator was crowded and slow. A clowder of kittens jammed the hallway, gossiping about the day's filming. Angel stopped to greet this one or that one, but her tail flicked back and forth in excitement.

Rushing by, she called over her shoulder, "Yes, hello," and "Yes, it was a good day," and "Yes, I'll talk to you later."

She needed to find Jazz, her roommate, and tell her the news.

As she was trotting away from the last group, a kitten's voice trailed after her: "Isn't she amazing? She's my cousin."

Angel's throat closed up. She should stop and chat with Hugo, should share her good news. His mother was MamaGrace's sister, so Angel had always known Hugo. But it was so hard to talk to anyone except Jazz. Probably no one would believe that she was shy, but she was honestly scared to share with the other kittens. She never knew what to say. Or not say.

A moment later, she burst into her dorm room. "Jazz! You'll never guess…"

Located on the west side of the building, their room had floor-to-ceiling windows, creating a light-filled space that welcomed her. Jazz, a Siamese kitten, twirled in front of the mirror. She was wearing a long ballerina's tutu made of fawn-colored netting. "Look!" Jazz said. "Miss Emily outdid herself this time!"

"It's lovely," said a black-and-white kitten.

Angel groaned to herself. Jazz had dragged home a stray kitten again. Angel had seen him before but couldn't quite remember his name, so she gave him a curt nod.

Tilting her head, Angel studied the new costume. As a dress-up cat, Jazz had a closet stuffed with clothing, something new almost every week. Her costumer, Miss Emily Doodle, sewed outfits that fit over Jazz's front legs, making her look like a miniature person with a gigantic kitten head. Jazz was only filmed from the front, not the side or back.

"Perfect!" Angel said. "But guess what!"

"Miss Emily has an expert eye for color," said the black-and-white kitten.

"Angel," Jazz said, "you know Rudy, don't you? We got to talking about costumes, and I wanted to show him this new one."

Angel looked him over. Rudy. She wouldn't forget his name again. His huge ears and black face made him look like a pixie. She remembered one of his videos now. His green eyes caught the viewer as he moved with adorable awkwardness. When he stumbled, the viewer wanted to catch and help him. His videos didn't do very well, though, for whatever reason. Angel thought he'd make a good piano cat since he was black and white to match the piano's keys.

"Where've you been, anyway?" Jazz asked. "It's almost dinnertime." She started pulling off the ballerina costume. "And I'm hungry."

"I'm trying to tell you. I stopped to talk with the Director," Angel said, her heart thumping, dancing with excitement. She glanced at Rudy and wished that he weren't there, but she couldn't wait another second.

Angel tapped at the computer on the desk, pulling up KittyTube. "I've had a lot of third-place videos," she said.

"I think," Rudy said, "you've had eight third-places."

"Actually, nine," Angel said. "But I've never had a second place or first place. Look!" She pointed to the number of views for kitten videos. Her "Flipping the Bully" video topped the list. At four months old, Angel had been working all her life to be in the top video.

Rudy's green eyes widened. "Wow! First place! Doesn't Jazz hold the record with five top videos?"

Angel flicked him an annoyed glance. This was her moment. Was he trying to spoil it?

But Jazz had the right reaction, saying, "Cool!" and then pouncing on Angel and roughing up her fur. They wrestled around, claws sheathed, but really putting strength into flipping each other or rolling over and over in a jubilant celebration.

Angel's heart swelled. Jazz was the right person to share her news with because she understood the excitement. And the terror that it would never happen again. Breathless, they stopped and began to groom their coats.

Rudy watched silently from under his long eyelashes, as if afraid to interrupt the moment.

Angel turned away and licked her paw, worried that Miss Tanya, her groomer, would be mad at the tangled hair tomorrow morning.

Jazz tapped the computer screen and pointed. "The views have shot up even more. It's doing well."

Angel grinned at her. "Hurrah!"

"Look!" Rudy crowded between Jazz and Angel. "Lots of comments too. And shares."

Jazz nodded. "Your reputation is growing. You're on a roll."

A thrill ran down Angel's spine, and she shivered delicately. "Do you think so? I work so hard! But really, this isn't my best video. It's only the one that got more views."

Jazz deliberately sat on her haunches to lick her paws.

Angel sighed. When Jazz did that, she was avoiding talking about something. "Okay," Angel said, "tell me."

Jazz stretched like a rubber band full of energy. She looked sideways at Angel.

"Go on," Angel said. "You won't stop till you tell me."

"Well, yesterday you were so worried about views that you were thinking about a new role," Jazz said. "Maybe Underdog Cat will work out for a while longer."

Angel leaped and batted at Jazz's face. But she kept her claws sheathed, just playing. "Underdog Cat always saves the day! She'll live forever!"

Jazz swatted back. "Yes. And yes, you work hard. You deserve it." She hesitated. "But does it make you happy? You just work and come back and sleep. You don't have enough friends."

Angel blinked. A pure white Persian, she had odd-colored eyes, one blue and one copper. When she blinked on camera, it was to do a soul-connect with the audience. But now she blinked in surprise. "You're my friend." She waved a paw at Rudy. "He's my friend. Aren't you?"

"Um, yeah. Of course," Rudy stammered.

Jazz's blue eyes blazed in her dark face. "No, it's not enough."

Angel grimaced, her insides quivering. Jazz was right. She should've shared her excitement at getting a top video with the others in the hallway. But how do you say that to someone? Rudy would likely never get a top video, so why would he be excited for her? The life of every kitten in the dorm was ruled by views.

It wasn't fair. But it was their life as KittyTubers.

Somehow, she couldn't share about ranking number one because she knew she wasn't better than anyone else. Only luckier. The number of views ruled their lives, but Angel wished she could just be an actor without worrying about the views. She got swept up in the rankings like any other kitten. But really she just wanted to be a superb actor. She only cared about the views because they meant she could keep on doing what she loved—acting. In the process, though, she didn't need to hurt anyone else's feelings. No, she couldn't share her good news. She didn't trust others to care. Because if she were them, she'd be jealous.

Besides, she was only as good as her next video. If the next one flopped, she was nothing.

A bell sounded in the hallway, the dinner bell.

Jazz hung the ballerina costume on a clothing stand. "Come on, O Famous One. I'm hungry. After dinner, the Director needs everyone to come to the Blue Room on the eighth floor. Are you ready, Rudy?"

Angel hung back while Jazz and Rudy left together, a self-assured Siamese kitten and a hopeful Devon Rex kitten. If only Angel could be more like Jazz, making friends so easily.

Reluctantly, Angel scampered after them. The corridor was empty now, the other kittens gone to the cafeteria. Angel shivered. Was her life empty too?

The Deadline

**JUST KITTEN
AROUND** Joke
Q: Where do kittens go on field trips?
A: Mew-seums!

"Eighth floor," called Mr. Sean, the elevator operator. A tall man with freckled skin, he was so scrawny that when he turned sideways, he almost disappeared. But he had a booming voice that echoed through the elevator lobby. "Exercise studios and the Blue Room."

When Majestic Kennels was built, the only elevators available had controls at a convenient height for humans. No cat could reach the control buttons. When an operator wasn't available, a stool was dragged into the elevator and positioned before the buttons. When needed, the kittens could climb the stool and punch a button for the correct floor. But it was easier when there was a human elevator operator.

When the Director called a meeting for all twenty-seven kittens, the elevator was always crowded.

Smashed into the back of the elevator, Angel heard Jazz say, "Thank you, Mr. Sean."

They'd eaten a fast dinner of fresh fish, interrupted by other kittens stopping by to congratulate Angel on getting the top video.

Now the press of kittens rushed forward, almost blocking the elevator doors. Angel cringed and wished she'd taken the stairs.

Finally Angel stepped off the elevator, the last kitten out. "Thank you, Mr. Sean."

He nodded and reached to push the Close Doors button.

Slouching in the doorway of the Blue Room, Angel studied the layout. They'd never met here before, and she wondered what the Director had planned. The ceilings were about twenty feet tall, double height. The room must go up into the ninth-floor space. Floor-to-ceiling glass ran along the wall next to the hallway, but the other three walls were bright blue. Well lit, the room was cheerful. Maybe too cheerful, Angel thought. It wasn't a room for relaxing. No kittens were lying down; instead, they roamed, groups forming and reforming as questions ran through the crowd. Why did the floor have blue mats? What was that pile of orange squares? They looked like sleeping pads, but not comfortable ones. What surprises did the Director have for them tonight?

Rudy chatted to another Devon Rex named Maria and a Singapura kitten named Curly. The three of them were the smallest kittens of the year, the pocket kittens.

By the opposite wall stood Quincy and PittyPat, Angel's brother and sister. Angel felt a well of joy at seeing them. She missed being with them daily, but she loyally watched every one of their videos. A black Persian, Quincy did well with food videos. PittyPat, a golden Persian, loved water videos. Angel didn't understand why a kitten would want to specialize in food videos or water videos. Eating spiders? Yuck. Swimming in a bathtub? Not for her.

She joined them, putting the blue mats between her and Rudy. They greeted each other by rubbing noses. PittyPat and Quincy lived on the tenth floor, too, like the other kittens. Angel seldom saw them, though, because everyone had busy videotaping schedules. Angel's nose wrinkled at Quincy because he smelled like canned tuna. He had probably taped a food video with tuna that morning. PittyPat smelled like soap, probably because she'd taken yet another bath on-camera. Angel needed to spend more time her brother and sister!

"Have you been up to the penthouse lately?" Quincy asked. That was where their parents lived.

"No," Angel said. "But I met MamaGrace for catnip tea yesterday. DaddyAlbert's film, *Puss and Boots*, should come out next month."

"I'm meeting MamaGrace tomorrow at the marina," PittyPat said. "You know that restaurant that serves fresh fish—"

Just then, the Director walked in. He was a scrawny sphynx cat, and he ruled Majestic Kennels with an iron paw. He wasted no time getting started.

"Yowza! I'm talking acrobatics," the Director said. His voice was almost drowned out by the twenty-seven kittens. He might be small, but he spoke with a big voice.

Bellowing even louder, he said, "Listen!"

Silence.

Rudy squealed.

The Director boomed again, "Listen."

"She pushed me!" Rudy pointed a paw at Maria, who scowled.

The Director glared at the kittens. Maria looked away, but Rudy crouched into a tiny ball, shivering. No one else moved.

With the room quiet, the Director settled back to all four feet, his hairless skin wrinkling into odd folds. "As you may know, this is an important month for KittyTube. It's ratings month. That means every studio will be tracked for total views. Majestic Kennels has been the top studio for three years, with the highest advertising rates. We need that advertising money to survive. That's why you'll find new leaderboards set up outside my office tomorrow. They will update hourly. For Majestic Kennels to earn more views than other kennels, each of you must have more views."

Angel felt like a balloon was inflating inside her, and she was about to burst. *How much more can I do to get views?*

"On the leaderboard, you'll be able to see where you rank within Majestic Kennels and against other kennels. Why does this matter?"

Angel knew what was coming and shivered.

The Director narrowed his eyes and glared at each clump of kittens, stretching the moment out as he looked all around the room. "At the end of the month, we must start cutting this year's class. We'll go from twenty-seven kittens to only twenty."

The kittens mewed softly, their voices hopeful, although no one said, "Choose me!" out loud.

The Director continued, his voice harsh, "And at the end of the next month, we have a new deadline. By then, we must cut to just ten. The top kittens will get a year's contract. The rest will need to find other work."

Gloom descended on the kittens. Looking around, no one would meet Angel's eyes. They'd known about this deadline all along. They all knew that the Kennels only allowed ten kittens added to the pool of KittyTube's actors each year. Only ten kittens would earn that right. What would the other seventeen kittens do? Four weeks before the axe fell.

Angel wanted to withdraw into herself, to curl into a ball and hide from the coming deadline. MamaGrace said that most kittens who were cut would find work within the kennels, doing things such as editing film, handling props, or marketing.

Angel unsheathed her claws, then retracted them. Her claws came out again and went back in. Claws. Pull them back. She just wanted to act. If she was cut as an actor...

The Director's voice interrupted her thoughts. "And last, I have an announcement. Yowza! Starting today, Majestic Kennels is providing you with an acrobatics class. This is an optional class, an experiment," he said. "But we have plans for anyone brave enough to finish the class. Let me

Flipping Out

Atfer the Director's introduction, a brown-skinned woman in camouflage pants and a T-shirt stepped forward. Her mouth was set in a grim line. Straight black hair framed her petite face. Angel tried not to gasp in surprise. The face was scarred on one side—like MamaGrace's face. Angel's mother had been injured in a car wreck two years before. She limped and wore an eye patch to hide the vacant eye socket. Angel wondered how the acrobatics teacher had gotten her scars.

"Sir, is this thing working?" The woman held up a small box that hung around her neck on a lanyard.

"The translator is working great," the Director said.

Most humans wore an earpiece for the cat-to-human speech translator, and Angel never paid attention. She took it for granted that humans and cats understood each other.

"Would you explain it to me?" Captain Piper said. "Does it translate human speech to cat meows? Or cat to human?" She let the box fall to

her chest and leaned forward to hear because the kittens were making a racket again.

Angel shook her head knowingly; everything about how the translator worked was secret. The Director wouldn't answer that question directly.

"You'll hear human speech," the Director said, "and we'll hear cat. Awesome, isn't it?"

"But…"

The Director waved toward the restless kittens. "You need to start the class."

Captain Piper straightened, her back suddenly rigid. "Quiet!" Her voice wasn't loud and bossy like the Director's, but it instantly caught the kittens' attention. It was the voice of authority. Captain Piper rocked back and forth, as if eager to begin. "Clear out the center of the room. Line up along the walls."

Obedient, the kittens scattered to the walls. Across from Angel, Rudy pushed his way to sit beside Jazz. On Angel's side of the room, PittyPat, and Quincy sat beside her.

Captain Piper walked to one corner of the room, where she stood looking around. "Here's what I can do," she said. She took off her translator necklace and zipped it into a pocket of her camo pants.

Distracted by her friends, Angel was startled by Captain Piper's run. Turning to watch, she gaped when the captain did a roundoff back handspring. Not that Angel—or any other kitten—knew what to call it then.

Captain Piper danced, pirouetted, flipped, and jumped her way from one side of the room to the other. She flew through the air in impossible ways.

Angel didn't know many humans. There was the red-faced Mr. Danny who helped the Director. Miss Tanya, dainty and neat, with long fingers and red nail polish, groomed Angel's fur coat. Camera operators were always around, and of course, and there were elevator operators. But Angel had no idea the human body could do such things. She hadn't meant to gasp, to hold her breath—scared that Captain Piper might stumble or fall—or to be so captivated by the movement. Its flow. Its grace. What had the Director called this? Acrobatics?

Finally Captain Piper stopped. Breathing hard, she put her translator back on and said, "That's what a human can do. I've been challenged with finding out what a cat's body can do. Can you do any of these acrobatics? Or something even more wonderful?"

More wonderful? Angel didn't know if that was possible. Could cat bodies do any of the acrobatics moves?

She thought of when Wesley, the huge Maine coon cat, fell off a table. He twisted in the air this way and that before landing on his feet. Cats always land on their feet. But if he needed to, could he control his body? Could he jump off a high place and turn with a flourish to make it a thing of beauty? And still land on his feet?

Angel was nodding, eager for new challenges and skills.

Captain Piper said, "Let's start with something easy. I need you to try a forward roll." She sat on the floor on her knees, tucked her head, and rolled forward.

"Try it," she commanded.

Angel sat on her hind legs and tucked her head. She tried to roll, but her legs stuck out awkwardly. She scrabbled for a foothold so she could push off. Pulling her legs tighter to her body helped, but when she bent forward, her head was on her tail. She pulled her tail to the back and finally rolled forward. The roll was crooked. To stand, she had to flop onto her side and then push up. But it was a roll.

She looked around. No one else had budged.

PittyPat stared at her with wide eyes, while Quincy avoided her gaze by looking at the ceiling.

Looking across the room, Angel tilted her head at Jazz in question. Jazz gave her a brief head shake; no. Angel had seen that straight-mouth look before. Jazz wasn't going to try anything.

Captain Piper's mouth was straight too, her voice tight. "Only one kitten brave enough to try it?" she asked.

Rudy tucked his head and rolled. He went crooked too, but he came up gloating, "I did it!"

"Only two brave kittens?" Captain Piper's voice deepened to a challenge.

Angel glared at her brother and sister, but they ignored her. Acrobatics was different, sure, but they tried fresh things for their videos all the time. Still, this felt more different, more foreign. Acrobatics excited her, but apparently not the others.

The Director had retreated to a corner to observe. Now he took a step forward to catch everyone's attention, his tail flicking nervously. "This is an optional class, as I said. Yowza! But I expect everyone to try everything today. You don't have to come back, but tonight, you work."

When the Director said, "Work," everyone worked.

With grunts, groans, and meows, the kittens tried the forward roll. Most fell sideways, awkward and angry. Angel tried several more times and finally managed one that felt almost straight.

Captain Piper tapped Angel's head. "You. Come out here."

Angel followed her to the middle of the room. Rudy was there too. She held her head high, proud that she'd been the first to try the forward rolls.

"What are your names?" Captain Piper asked. "And what cat breed are you? I'm still learning."

"I'm Angel, a Persian."

"I'm Rudy, a Devon Rex."

"When you do a forward roll," Captain Piper said, "it's important to push off equally from both feet." She shouted to the room, "Watch these two do the forward roll." She motioned to Rudy and Angel.

Angel sat on her hind legs, pulled her tail out of the way, tucked and rolled. Following what Captain Piper said, she concentrated on pushing off equally with both hind legs. The roll felt smoother than before. It was interesting to pay attention to her body like this. To do the roll correctly, she had to be aware of how her legs and tail and head all worked together.

But she still had trouble landing on her feet, falling sideways at the end of the roll. Rudy sprawled awkwardly too.

Good, she thought. *It's not just me.*

Captain Piper said, "Those are not beautiful forward rolls, but they're a start. If you practice, you'll get better." She waved to the room. "Each of you try ten more rolls. If you need me to watch or to help, I'll be walking around."

Jazz raised a paw. "Captain Piper, I can't seem to go over."

Captain Piper nodded. "I'll give you a slight push to help you feel how it works."

Angel was left in the middle of the floor with Rudy. She raised an eyebrow. "Do you want to learn this stuff?"

"Yeah!" Rudy said. "I'll be here tomorrow."

Too bad Rudy was interested too. She was a superfeline, the Underdog Cat. But Rudy always acted like an underdog. They just didn't see the world the same way.

Angel sighed. She hoped a clowder of kittens would show up for acrobatics. But either way, she was in.

EPISODE 2
Armadillo Attack

The armadillo waves his nose in the air. Half-blind, he can only see a few inches ahead. Smelling helps him find his way around.

He stops. His face waggles from side to side, searching. There.

On a stone sits a metal bowl full of food. The camera doesn't focus on the food, so it could've been fish or earthworms or dry cat food. It doesn't matter. What matters is the play of shadows, bright sun filtering through the thick leaves of a towering oak. A kitten hides in the flickering shadows, a study in black and white himself.

Rudy stretches to reach over the top lip of the bowl and snatches a bite. He pulls back into the shadows, sitting on his haunches and chewing.

Suddenly, the armadillo charges.

The kitten freezes. His green eyes glimmer with fear.

Never fear!

Underdog Cat flies to the rescue.

(Really, she leaps from a tree limb. On video, it just looks like she's been flying around looking for someone who needs help.)

She lands on the armadillo's back and digs in her claws. Except the armadillo's armor is too tough for her claws. The armadillo bucks like a wild horse, and Underdog Cat flies into the food bowl, knocking it over and spilling—oh, it's dry cat food.

Underdog Cat scrambles up and leaps at the armadillo. This time, her claws find the brute's sensitive nose.

(Earlier they'd practiced the stunt. When Angel pats his nose, Herman, the armadillo, just has to react the right way. The camera will make it look like she scratches him.)

The armadillo squeals and curls into a ball.

Underdog Cat waits, back arched, hissing.

Peering out from under his armor, the armadillo shivers. In a swift movement, he uncurls and dashes away.

Rudy inches up to Underdog Cat, who stares up at the tree. Finally she glances down at him.

Rudy gazes up at her. "Thank you," his emerald eyes say. "You saved the day."

Again.

Lunch With Rudy and Jazz

"Tha" was great." Rudy danced around Angel, trying to keep in front of her so he could talk to her.

Cringing, Angel turned away, trotting toward the elevator.

"Let's go to lunch. Are you going to the cafeteria? We can talk about the filming. Herman did an impressive job, didn't he? Was it hard to climb the oak tree? Was it scary to jump like that? Were you scared you'd miss him?"

Angel sighed. Rudy was nice enough, but she didn't need his endless chatter. "No, I've got to find Jazz."

"Oh. Why?"

Angel wanted to sneak away alone, not answer his questions. But she was too polite to ignore a direct question. "Well, Jazz and I always eat lunch together."

"Cool!" Rudy said. "Maybe I can join you?"

Angel didn't answer. She wondered how she could get away from Rudy and find Jazz by herself.

She liked their quiet lunches, when they shared about their morning's work.

Mr. Sean, the elevator operator, called, "Fifth floor, Studios 10 to 15. Going up."

"Let's go!" Rudy scampered toward the elevator.

Since the cafeteria was on the ninth floor, Angel had no choice but to follow.

A human hurried off the elevator, carrying a basket full of grooming supplies: combs, brushes, a hair dryer, ribbons, and bows. *There must be an emergency on some set*, Angel thought.

As Angel and Rudy stepped inside, Mr. Sean said, "Good morning, Miss Persian. Mr. Devon Rex."

They nodded politely at him.

Rudy picked up their conversation, saying, "Do you think our video will go viral? That would be so great, because I really need a boost."

Sighing, Angel wondered why Rudy was even in her Underdog Cat video. Was she supposed to pull up his views? "How old are you, anyway?" she asked.

"Sixteen weeks," Rudy said.

"That's my age," Angel said. "Why are you still an innocent? Every other kitten has moved on."

"Because Devons are so little," he said. "We can stay innocents for years. My uncle was an innocent for three years before he found a new role."

Angel grimaced. "That's not fair."

"It's not fair or unfair. It just is," Rudy said. "The Maine coon kittens were giants at birth and never got to be innocents, while I'm as small as a mouse. It's just who we are."

"Innocent was so easy," Angel said wistfully.

"You think it's easy to stay an innocent?" Rudy's voice rose. "To appear naive, like I know nothing? It takes as much acting as for you to be Underdog Cat." He lifted his chest and head and looked away.

"Ninth floor, cafeteria. Going up," Mr. Sean said.

Angel and Rudy stepped off the elevator.

Just outside the cafeteria stood Jazz, surrounded by a small clowder. TyAdam was an American shorthair who was rumored to be a good mouser, though maybe it was just his grandfather who still ate wild meat. Rhapsody was a charming Norwegian Forest cat with overlong hairs coming out of her ears. Angel had always wondered if they were antennae to catch the Wi-Fi. She looked away from Isobelle, an exotic cat. Angel and Isobelle were both white cats, so sometimes they had to work together. Angel didn't like to be compared to

Isobelle, because Angel had such different grooming needs. She was groomed daily, while Isobelle's hair was easily managed with a light grooming. *We aren't the same at all*, Angel thought.

"Angel. Rudy. Are you going in to eat?" Jazz asked. "Let's sit together."

Angel's heart sank. After a hard morning on the set, she didn't want a crowd like this. She was so tired of Rudy's chatter and excitement. But she didn't want to eat alone either. She wished she could be more like Jazz, friends with everyone.

Enthusiastic, Rudy bounded to Jazz and rubbed her cheek with his. "You won't believe how hard we worked..."

Sighing, Angel followed the clowder of kittens into the cafeteria. With Jazz and Rudy around, she needed to get used to crowds.

The Doodle Studio

Miss Emily sat on the floor, cross-legged, and leaned toward the stool where Jazz stood. Angel watched with fascination as the designer fitted a new costume onto Jazz's body. Because Jazz was still a growing kitten, each costume was a custom fit and could only be worn for a month before Jazz outgrew it. Miss Emily had a mouthful of long, straight pins. She pinched fabric around Jazz's front leg and pushed in a pin.

"Ouch!" Jazz yelled.

Angel winced in sympathy.

"Sorry," Miss Emily said. "Just don't move, or it could be worse."

Jazz sucked in a sharp breath, held it and stilled her body. Miss Emily's hair was mostly in a long braid down her back, but frizzy hair escaped to curl around her face. She looked like a fairy-tale Snow White with ebony hair, ivory skin, and deep red lips. Only her hands showed that she worked as a clothing designer, with dry pin-pricked skin.

The Director usually chose designers for well-known stars. One way for a designer to break in was to design for a kitten. If the kitten did well, the

designer would do well. When Jazz's parents chose Miss Emily, she was unknown. Jazz's unexpected success also meant success for the Doodle Studio.

Angel had come with her roommate to give her opinion on costumes. But Jazz didn't need much advice. Instead, Angel stood in the window of Miss Emily's loft studio, watching the boat docks below. There were twenty berths for large river barges. New barges came and went daily because they brought in most of the supplies and goods for Kittywood. The city was built in a forgotten valley somewhere in North America. No roads connected to Kittywood, so it was supplied only by river barges or helicopters. When a barge pulled into the dock, people swarmed to unload it. Tall cranes swung bulky containers to shore. While she watched, they reloaded one barge with containers and unloaded another.

"Angel," called Miss Emily, "what do you think of this?"

Angel turned back to the studio to look at Jazz's costume. A gold circlet with a triangular medallion went around Jazz's head. As usual, Miss Emily had added human arms to the costume to make Jazz appear as a miniature person. This time the human arms had metal cuffs from the wrist to the elbow. Tall red boots completed the blue, gold, and red costume. Jazz had become a superfeline, Wonder Cat.

"Wow!" Angel said. "It's a winner."

Miss Emily stood back and tilted her head from side to side. "It works." She waved at a mirror. "Jazz, are you happy with it?"

Nodding, Jazz said, "Purr-fect. Let's get it off so you can finish it. Will you send it later today so I can tape tomorrow?"

"Yes, I'll have it done before the end of the day." Miss Emily helped Jazz remove the costume. She set it on a cutting table that held stacks of fabric. Along one wall stood sewing machines of various kinds, from embroidery machines to regular sewing machines to huge quilting machines. Another wall had shelves with clear boxes of trims, laces, and buttons.

Turning to Angel, Miss Emily said, "I've been wanting to make a cape. Jazz's costume doesn't need one, though. Have you ever thought about giving Underdog Cat a cape?"

"No." Angel stepped backward, then paused. Jazz was always in the top three videos on the leaderboard. Maybe adding a costume was a good idea. Would a cape push her from number three to number two? Or even number one again?

"What a splendid idea!" Jazz said. "Angel, I know you wouldn't wear the costumes I do. But a cape—well, it's not fitted like my costumes. It would just add some visual action when you move. It would be adorable! You could do a test video with one and see what you think."

"No!" Her voice squeaked, full of uncertainty. Why did everyone call her adorable? She wanted to be dangerous. And even if she was adorable, so what? There were lots of adorable but dangerous animals: hippopotamuses, blue-ringed octopuses, and polar bears. *Cats can be dangerous too*, she thought.

From a stack of fabric, Miss Emily pulled out a length of burgundy satin. "This might do." She grabbed a tape measure and started toward Angel. "Let me just measure you…"

"No!" Angel backed up until, surprised, she bumped into the window.

"Oh, I didn't mean to startle you," Miss Emily said. She sank to the floor and crossed her legs, keeping her eyes on Angel. Talking softly, she said, "It's all right. I know it's strange to have someone touch you and measure you. You're such a lovely Persian. That white fur needs a satin, something as soft as you are."

Angel stared, listening to Miss Emily's gentle voice. She closed her eyes and tried to picture herself doing the Underdog Cat videos while wearing a cape. Adorable, but dangerous. She could still leap and duck. A cape wouldn't stop her from rolling, would it?

Would her audience like her in a cape? Did she need it?

And would it help her ratings? That was the real question.

All the while, Miss Emily talked softly. Puzzled, Angel realized she was purring. Miss Emily's voice had soothed and calmed her.

But Angel had to be practical. She opened her eyes and stared at Miss Emily. "How much will it cost?"

"For you? Nothing, because it's just a simple cloak. If you like it, come back for other costumes, and we'll figure out the costs then," Miss Emily said. "Does that work?"

Jazz said, "She always creates samples for kittens to try out. You should do this, Angel."

Did Underdog Cat need a cape? Angel didn't think so, but maybe it wouldn't hurt to try. It might be good to experiment.

She took a deep breath and said, "Don't stick me with a pin."

Need To Know

HAHAHA

JUST KITTEN
AROUND Joke

Q. There were four cats in a boat, and one jumped out. How many were left?

A. None. They were all copycats!

Fifth floor! Stages 10 to 15. Going up," Mr. Sean said.

Angel shook her head. "Going down," she said. "I'll wait for you to come back."

"Again?" Mr. Sean tugged at his uniform, which ballooned around him.

Angel shrugged, embarrassed.

When the elevator doors clanged shut, Angel paced back and forth in front of the doors, waiting for it to stop again on its way down.

She shouldn't check the leaderboard again. For the fifth time that day. But it updated hourly. She just needed to know where her video stood. Her "Armadillo Attack" video had held third place all day. She hoped it would climb to second place. But Jazz's video as Wonder Cat was climbing the boards too. She was on a roll. And Quincy had a great food video. She didn't think the armadillo would beat Quincy, but maybe it could beat out the superfeline. Maybe.

The elevator dinged, and the doors opened.

Mr. Sean said, "Fifth floor! Stages 10 to 15. Going down."

Angel avoided looking at Mr. Sean and stepped onto the elevator, tail held high. She found herself face-to-face with Rudy.

"Good afternoon," Rudy said in a squeaky voice. "Where are you going?"

"Um, downstairs."

"Me too. I need to check the leaderboard." Rudy bounced on his toes. "Isn't it exciting? Someone told me that the armadillo video is in the top five. I've never been in the top five before."

Above him, Mr. Sean raised a shaggy eyebrow.

Angel looked away, her stomach clenching in frustration. The Director was boosting Rudy's career by putting him in Angel's video. In fact, videos for the top stars all included a lower-ranked kitten right now. The Director was making a smart move, trying to boost everyone's career, and she hoped it worked. But it also irked her. Her work was being used to support someone else. Shouldn't they earn it by themselves?

"First floor. The Director's office and Majestic Kennels Visitors' Center," Mr. Sean said. "Going up."

Angel and Rudy exited and turned directly left toward the west wing of the building, where the Director's office was located. As they neared the west wing lobby, a murmur of meows grew louder and louder.

The lobby area was brightly lit with enormous windows that looked out onto a lawn enclosed by a privacy fence. That's where they had set up the stage for Angel's first snow video. It had only been two months ago, but it felt like years. The snow angel video still received a ton of views, maybe from people who were already tired of warmer weather.

The reception area had white marble floors, cold under her paws. Colorful pillows for cats leaned against the windows, and comfortable chairs for humans scattered the area. Wall-mounted TV monitors displayed the leaderboard. Or, rather, boards. The first board was for the leaders of any video, whether cats or kittens. The stars of KittyTube dominated it: Albert Persian, Wesley Maine Coon, and rising stars like Kathleen Ragdoll. The second board—the only one that Angel cared about—listed lead videos for kittens. The third board showed the overall scores for the five big kennels: Majestic

Kennels, Cardinal Kennels, Fox Kennels, Malachi-Glenys Kennels, and Wells Brothers Kennels.

Red letters on a black background and rows of numbers that would determine her fate—Angel cringed. But she stiffened her spine and stalked toward the board. The digital clock beside the leaderboard read 3:58 p.m. The board updated exactly at the top of the hour, so they had two minutes to wait. An eternity.

Angel looked around and recognized several kittens. Rudy had strolled off, talking to one kitten and then another. Angel glanced up. 3:59 p.m. One minute till updated rankings.

She retreated across the room to a quiet spot, not wanting to be in the mix of kittens when the numbers flipped. Her stomach ached from the tension. She shook herself from nose to tail tip. She needed to relax and not worry about this. But what if...

The red letters and numbers flickered, updating, updating, updating. Finally they settled into new letters and numbers.

Number one on the kittens' leaderboard: Quincy's latest food video, "Kitten Smorgasbord."

Angel agreed that it was a great video. Quincy walked up and down a long table loaded with food. He sampled everything from a roasted suckling pig to the wings of a tiny squab. At the end, he lay on a golden platter, showing off his fat belly, and slept. She couldn't wait to congratulate him. This was his second video to hit number one.

Number two on the kittens' leaderboard: Jazz's Wonder Cat video. Jazz would be thrilled. So cool.

Number three on the kittens' leaderboard: "Armadillo Attack."

So. Third place.

Still.

Nothing had changed all day.

The clock read 4:02 p.m.

Angel sighed. Fifty-eight minutes till the next update. Maybe she could come down for the 5:00 p.m. update. She closed her eyes against the red letters, but an afterglow still showed up on the back of her eyelids. Third place.

She opened her eyes. 4:03 p.m. Only fifty-seven minutes till the next update.

Without waiting for Rudy, she turned back to the main lobby. There, she shoved open a doorway marked Stairway. Angel didn't want to see Mr. Sean again. He would just make comments. Because Angel *would* come back at 5:00 p.m. She needed to know the score. Every hour, she needed to know.

Underdog Cat vs. Coyote

— · ★ · —

The sun hangs like a red ball on the horizon. A tiny black-and-white kitten stops at a crossroad. In one direction, the path is wide and is lit by streetlights. The other path narrows and darkens, leading through trees. The trail looks like a cave with a pinprick of light at the other end.

The light is a grocery store.

Pulling back, the camera shows a clump of bushes and there—quivering—is a slender nose. The kitten doesn't see that nose.

The kitten stares down the wide, well-lit street. His head moves, tracing out a square in midair. You can see him thinking, *That's the long way around.* His eyes widen, and he shakes his head. *No.*

Turning, the kitten looks down the narrow, dark path. His pink tongue licks his upper lip. He's hungry. Maybe the grocery store has fish skeletons out back in its dumpster. He needs to eat. He licks his lip again.

From the bushes, sharp black eyes flash at the kitten.

But the kitten doesn't see those eyes, those deep, dark eyes and glinting teeth. Something else is hungry too.

The kitten only thinks about fish bones. Gathering himself, the kitten dashes down the dark path.

Suddenly a black form rises from the shadows. The foolish kitten stops, skidding a few feet. He backs up, but the creature stalks him.

Step by step.

The kitten backs away, stumbles, then scrambles up to back away again, not daring to take his eyes off his stalker.

It's a coyote!

Silhouetted against the light, it's one colossal coyote. A crafty coyote. A hungry coyote!

"Help!" cries the kitten. "Help!"

(Cue: Underdog Cat music begins softly but gets louder through the rest of this episode.)

(Camera: Pull back to the entrance to the dark path.)

Underdog Cat hurtles down the narrow path, blue cape billowing behind her. When she leaps over the kitten, her feet tangle in the cape. She falls, rolling and wrapping herself in blue, and tumbles into the coyote like a crazy blue ball.

The coyote stumbles backward, biting at the blue cape.

Underdog Cat kicks frantically, blinded by blue. Her front leg pops free. She unsheathes her claws and strikes wildly, hoping to hit something. There. She scratches something.

The coyote yelps, and blood spurts from a small cut on his nose. He rubs his nose on the cape, leaving a stain of red. He turns and trots away, his tail tucked between his legs.

(Off-camera, a stage manager rushes in to wipe the red food coloring off Stephen's nose. Stephen smirks at Underdog Cat, who's still wrestling with the silly cape. A cape! What was Angel thinking?)

Underdog Cat finally frees another leg and stands. She tosses her head, trying to position the cape on her back. Instead, it hangs awkwardly in front of her. She needs to walk but can't because the cape's ties are now at the back of her neck where she can't reach them, can't untie them.

The black-and-white kitten looks up at Underdog Cat with adoring eyes that seemed to say, "How can I thank you? You saved my life!"

Fortunately, the episode ends on that note, with a full view of the adoring kitten.

The Underdog Cat video ends without another look at the embarrassed Underdog Cat.

Family Night

When MamaGrace and DaddyAlbert invite their kittens to supper, you know it's going to be a hilarious night.

First, MamaGrace will cook—
well, she doesn't cook,
but she orders in with flair!—
and the food will be delicious
unless she forgets
that Quincy is allergic to shrimp.
(He learned the hard way
in one of his food videos,
not one the Director allowed
to be shown on KittyTube,
thank goodness.)
Fortunately, Quincy reminds her.
So she cancels the shrimp order,
and everyone looks at each other
thinking, *What now? I'm hungry.*
Then PittyPat arrives, bringing
Chinese carry-out—
KungKitty Chicken

is raw chicken
with peppers,
forget the rice—
and the family loses themselves
in nibbling, munching, and chomping,
until Angel is stuffed
and asks MamaGrace and DaddyAlbert,
"What have you been doing lately?"
They launch into a lengthy explanation
of videos and teaching acting—interrupted
by PittyPat asking about this,
and Quincy asking about that,
and Angel asking about the same things again
(about whom MamaGrace was teaching,
and who was the director
of DaddyAlbert's new videos,
and other details about the life of a KittyTuber,
like leaderboards,
and how to hit number one again and again,
and how to stay upbeat)—
and mostly, just laughing and chatting
 and laughing.
Then MamaGrace says,
"What have you been doing lately?"
And each kitten describes
acting problems,
Director problems,

friend problems,

Director problems,

(Yowza! Did I say, Director problems?)

and MamaGrace and DaddyAlbert hang on
each word

and exclaim and laugh, cry and meow,

about the minor problems

(or not-so-small Director problem)

until the family

feels all caught up

and stuffed full of takeout chicken

and loved and loved and all connected again

(and did I say, they feel loved?)

and it's late,

too late for kittens to be out.

So the kittens must go back downstairs

to sleep in the kittens' dorm

on the tenth floor,

knowing that

MamaGrace and DaddyAlbert

are there

in the penthouse.

And all is well,

because MamaGrace loves them

and DaddyAlbert loves them

and they are a family

and will always be a family.

And always, always
will be loved.

The Kennels' Leaderboard

The Director insisted on publishing the "Underdog Cat vs. Coyote" video on KittyTube. "Every kitten needs a video every week," the Director said. "No weeks off. I'm sorry you don't like the video, but if you don't let me publish it, you'll get zero new views for the week. Remember, we're cutting from twenty-seven kittens to twenty. You need some views, even if it's not many."

Angel hid in her room for three days. She slashed at the red-food-coloring-stained cape until it was shredded, and then she shoved it down the trash chute. She refused to turn on her computer to watch anyone else's videos.

Jazz tried to talk. "Your video has…"

But Angel clapped her paws over her ears and cried, "Go away!"

Angel was so mad—at herself.

Finally she had to get out of her room. She waited until Jazz left for supper and the hallway quieted;

KITTY TUBERS

1	**Jazz** *1,896,455*	**11**	**Rhapsody** *298,455*
2	**Rudy** *1,761,099*	**12**	**Angel** *256,999*
3	**PittyPat** *989,900*	**13**	**Casper** *249,555*
4	**Ty Adams** *876,900*	**14**	**Missy** *225,234*
5	**Maria** *699,084*	**15**	**Curly** *219,000*
6	**Patch** *566,954*	**16**	**Kathleen** *213,222*
7	**Yoshi** *499,268*	**17**	**Muffin** *198,000*
8	**Isobelle** *399,046*	**18**	**Wesley** *167,110*
9	**Oliver** *385,005*	**19**	**Blue** *155,500*
10	**Sassy** *300,004*	**20**	**Smokey** *130,300*

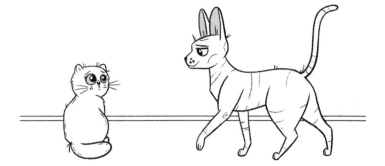

everyone else had gone to eat too. She opened the door and tiptoed to the elevator.

"Tenth floor. Kittens' dorm. Going down."

Angel stepped onto the elevator and wished for a place to hide. Instead, she backed into a corner and hoped no one else would get on.

Mr. Sean didn't speak on the way down, and Angel was glad for the silence.

"First floor. The Director's office and Majestic Kennels Visitors' Center," Mr. Sean said. "Going up."

Stepping off, Angel held her tail high. She tried not to think of the blue cape, but blue swam before her eyes.

She followed the west hallway, slinking from shadowed doorway to shadowed doorway. Fortunately, it was the middle of the hour, so no one was there waiting for the leaderboard to update.

The number one video was Jazz's Wonder Cat video, up from last week's number two spot.

Of course.

Angel scanned the list, cringing, yet hoping.

Number eleven: "Underdog Cat vs. Coyote."

Eleven. Angel sucked in air. What a relief! Respectable. Not in the top ten, but respectable.

Maybe she was safe. She closed her eyes and shook her head. *Safe.* She didn't want to be safe; she needed to be on top. The best.

"Angel, what are you doing here?"

At the somber voice, Angel opened her eyes and spun around. The Director stood in the doorway of his office, frowning. It's hard to say that a cat grins or frowns because they don't use their mouths like humans. Yet the Director definitely frowned, his mouth turned down at the corners.

"Just checking." Angel nodded at the leaderboard.

The Director walked across the lobby, claws clicking on the white marble. He studied the leaderboards. Waving a paw at the kittens' leaderboard, he said, "You watch that one. Do you ever study this leaderboard?" He looked up at the board that listed the kennels' rankings.

The red numbers cast a faint, eerie glow onto his head. Since sphynx cats are hairless, it made him look like he wore a red halo.

Angel shook her head. "No. I can't do anything about that one."

"Can't you?" the Director said. "Every video helps add to our reputation. We're still on top, but our lead is shrinking. Yowza! We used to lead by a million views or more when Albert Persian had a new video out. But now we only have a few thousand views as a lead."

Curious, Angel studied the boards. "Why has that changed?"

"Besides the fact that your dad moved on to full-length movies?" the Director said. "No, it's more than that. All the kennels have lots of talent. More cats mean more videos. More videos mean that yours has to stand out somehow. You need to act better than your mother ever did to get the same number of views as she did in those early years. KittyTube is growing up as a business."

Angel sat on her haunches and licked her front paw, thinking. It wasn't fair that she had to do better than MamaGrace or DaddyAlbert, who were the best ever. But they started in the early days of kitten kennels. Back when they named the video studios as kennels because they expected to add dogs to the videos. A cattery is a home for just cats, no dogs allowed. But a kennel can be a home for either dogs or cats. When they first started, they used "Kennel" in all the names so they had options if KittyTube didn't work out. Maybe they could try DoggyTube or PetTube. Fortunately, KittyTube took off. But "Kennel" had stuck.

She looked again at the kittens' board. This year's kittens, from all across Kittywood, worked here at

Majestic Kennels. It made sense to train them all together. Every kitten knew, though, which was their home kennel; and their kitten views counted for that home kennel. Because her parents worked for Majestic Kennels, Angel's views counted for them. Later, when they were offered a yearly contract, it might come from any kennel. She might get offers from two or three kennels. It would be strange to move over to Malachi-Glenys Kennels or Wells Brothers Kennels. But it could happen. And then she'd be worried about that kennel's ratings. She looked at the kennels' rankings with a new interest.

The Director was still talking. "I know you didn't like your blue cape video. You brought this on yourself by trying the cape without asking. I would've asked for a test video to find out how it worked for you. We always run a test for Jazz's costumes. Always. Every week."

Jazz had told her this. But Angel hadn't understood why they tested so much. It had seemed pointless to her. After the blue cape, she finally understood.

"But Majestic Kennels needs your views," the Director said. "See how far ahead we are this week? Now, look at your views. Your views, by themselves, puts Majestic Kennels in the lead. And that's when you're only number eleven on the kittens' list."

Amazed, Angel looked from the kittens' leaderboard to the kennels' leaderboard. The Director was right. Her views were enough to put Majestic Kennels ahead of the others. It was a slim lead. The kitten videos were more important than she'd thought.

Which was Jazz's studio? Wasn't she from Fox Kennels? So her number one views were keeping that kennel at the number two position? Interesting.

Still. That blue cape was awful.

"I'm sorry that I didn't ask," Angel said. She remembered unwrapping the cape and rubbing her face across the satin. So slick and smooth! She had hoped that it would turn around her fortunes, that she'd found a way to get the number one spot over and over. She shook her head. "I thought you'd say no."

The Director raised his front shoulders and let them drop heavily. "I'm open for change. I love new ideas. *If* they bring in views. Don't forget that next time. What I care about is the success of Majestic Kennels."

The Director didn't explain things often. Angel dared another question. "Is that why you put Rudy in my videos?"

"Of course," the Director said. "I have two jobs you know. I'm head of Majestic Kennels, but I also direct the kittens' dorm for all of Kittywood. I care about our kennel, but I balance that with making sure KittyTube does well overall."

Angel shook her head. She'd never thought about these things. She'd only paid attention to her own videos. It was fascinating to step back and take a wider view.

"You may not have noticed," the Director said, "but I've been pairing up kittens. All of them. For example, Quincy is working with Daniel Siamese, who's never taken off like his sister, Jazz. Next week, PittyPat will work with Hugo, your cousin, who needs a big boost in views. I'm trying to help the kittens with fewer views to get some attention. And it's working. Rudy's solo videos are doing a little better."

Angel nodded. Better, but not good enough. He was likely to be cut when they pruned the group from twenty-seven to twenty kittens.

"You know, Rudy would be a great piano cat," Angel said impulsively. "He's all black and white like the piano. Get a baby grand with a mirror behind the keys. Maybe shoot it in black and white."

The Director stared at her, his ears twitching above his bald head. "What an interesting idea!"

Angel barely heard his reaction because she was thinking again of her own views. Well, she had to.

The Director didn't care which twenty kittens made the next cut. He only cared that, overall, the kittens added a certain percentage to Majestic Kennels' views. She understood that he cared most about Majestic Kennels. That was his job.

But her job, her worry, was her own views.

Her own career.

Acrobatic Flips

Hey! I'm going to acrobatics," Angel said. Her tail twitched in anticipation. "Coming?"

"No." Jazz turned away, looking out the window. "It's not for me."

"It was fun." Angel had loved the challenge of moving her body in new ways. And she loved the idea of being in control of how her body moved. She hoped it would help her become a better actor, with more views.

Jazz rolled her eyes. "Not me. I'll get hurt."

Angel tilted her head, her odd-colored eyes studying her roommate. "We're different, aren't we?" It was deeper than just different cat breeds. On a basic level, they wanted and needed different things. They were willing to do different things to reach their goals.

"I'm happy with who I am," Jazz said.

"I'm never happy with me," Angel said. "I always need to find what's next."

"You push me to do things differently." Jazz sat awkwardly and tried to do a forward roll but couldn't push herself over. Panting, she said, "Even when I don't want to."

"It's easier," Angel said, "if you keep your tail behind you. But, okay. I get it. You don't have to come to acrobatics. But you're missing out."

"You can tell me all about it later." Jazz waved a paw at Angel, then turned to her closet. She started flipping through her clothes. At the end of every month, she cleaned out costumes she'd outgrown.

Angel took the stairs down the two flights to the eighth floor. The Blue Room had windows on the hallway, so she saw right away that everything was dark. Angel stepped through the doorway and called, "Hello?"

"Come in." Captain Piper, wearing camo leggings and a camo shirt, sat on a mat in the dark, stretching her legs.

Angel wondered if she ever wore color or if she always wanted to disappear into the background.

"Where is everyone?" Angel asked.

Captain Piper motioned at the empty room. "It looks like you're the only one still interested in acrobatics." She flopped back on the mat, spread-eagle, and sighed.

She's sad, Angel thought, *that no one else is interested. I'm sad too.*

"I'm interested." Rudy stood in the doorway, his shadow from the hallway lights reaching toward Captain Piper.

Angel sighed. She couldn't escape the little Devon.

Captain Piper stood, a smooth, graceful movement. "Fine." Her mouth was set in a hard line. "We'll do it with just two kittens."

"Is that enough?" Angel asked. She worried that acrobatics would end because no one showed up.

"I don't know." Captain Piper flipped on lights and trotted to a stack of foam cubes covered in orange fabric. She pulled several cubes to the room's center. They were large, about three feet tall and three feet wide. "The Director has some project in mind, but he hasn't told me what."

"Oh, I know about that," Angel said. "My groomer, Miss Tanya, said that Mr. Danny told her the Director got a call from a major movie director, asking for help." Why hadn't the Director told this to Captain Piper? Sometimes the Director liked to hold his cards too close to his chest.

"What kind of help?" Rudy asked. He climbed on the first cube and jumped off, landing lightly on all four feet. He spun around as if to say, "Look at me! This is fun!"

"They are asking if we can be stunt cats," Angel said. She leaped onto the cube too.

"What's a stunt cat?" Rudy said.

Captain Piper motioned for them both to climb up the cube stairs again.

Angel said, "Well, a regular cat, the ones outside Kittywood, the silent ones—"

"Cats outside Kittywood aren't silent," Captain Piper said. "They meow and make other noises."

"Sure," Angel said. "But we call them silent cats because they can't talk to humans like we can with our translation programs. Anyway, silent cats can be trained to do things. But the Hollywood directors wonder if a talking cat would be better for some roles. They want someone they can direct, instead of a cat they have to train."

"Today, I need you to jump from the cube," Captain Piper said. "But as you fall, try to do a forward roll in the air before you land on your feet."

"Like Captain Piper is directing us now," Rudy said.

Angel nodded. "Yes, exactly."

For the next hour, the two kittens practiced jumping from a cube, doing a single flip, and landing on their feet. It was surprisingly easy, except Captain Piper kept pushing them to control their bodies better. "Don't let your legs flop around," Captain Piper said. "Your body should be a clean line."

Rudy made noises when he jumped. He hummed, chirped, mewed, warbled, trilled, and sang. It drove Angel crazy.

"Stop that noise," she said.

Rudy tried to be quiet, but he just couldn't. Every jump, he stood atop the foam cube and told Angel, "This time, I'll be quiet."

Then he jumped and sang.

"You're weird," Angel told him.

Captain Piper kept adding a cube to force them to jump from a higher place. She built a stairway of cubes ending in the tallest tower of cubes. The stairway made it easy for the kittens to climb to the top. Each time, Angel and Rudy looked at each other in excitement.

Rudy said, "Ready?"

Angel yelled, "Jump!"

Angel easily controlled her body through the flip. Rudy sang as he flipped and landed upright.

At four cubes high, though, Angel said, "That's enough. I'm not jumping from anything higher." Four cubes put them at about twelve feet high, with the roof still another eight feet above them. They had ceiling room for more cubes, but Angel didn't think it would help her do the flips any better.

"Oh," Captain Piper said. Her eyebrows arched, pulling the scar on her face into an angry red color. "It is getting high for a small cat." She suddenly crossed her legs and sat.

Rudy stood beside her, grooming his belly with his tongue.

Angel lapped from a water bowl before coming back to Captain Piper. "What's wrong?"

"It would help if I knew which tricks they need you to do," she said. "I'm working blind here."

"No one knows what tricks we need, not even the Director. This is something new for video cats," Angel said. "So let's do basic tricks first. We can't put together a whole fight scene with acrobatics yet. We can only do one thing. Teach us the basics because that's the right thing to do." This was more fun than anything she was doing in her videos right now. She hoped she could use acrobatics in a video soon.

Rudy said, "I wonder if I could do a double flip? Is it hard?"

Captain Piper shrugged. "I don't know what cats can or can't do yet. Let's try it. You must flip faster. You'll travel the same distance from the top of the cube to the ground. But you'll want to do two flips. The only way that works is if you spin faster."

Rudy scampered up the cube stairway, followed by Angel. From the top, they looked at each other, eyes sparkling.

"Ready?" Rudy said.

Angel yelled, "Jump!"

Together they jumped, and Rudy sang.

The flips were wild and sloppy. Both landed on their feet, but neither had done a double.

Double flips! Wow, they were hard.

Videotaping of Angel Persian

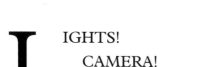

L IGHTS!
  CAMERA!
  ACTION!

stalking leaping	pose here
creeping crawling	pose there

CUT!
no, no, no

pose there	just there	
no, there	yes, there	there

MAKEUP!
LIGHTS!
CAMERA!
ACTION!

stalking leaping	pose here
creeping crawling	pose there
resting	move move?

MOVE!	move where?
CUT!	

Here	move
do this	do that
like this	like that

READY?

MAKEUP!
LIGHTS!
CAMERA!
ACTION!

stalking leaping	pose here
creeping crawling	pose there
(pausing pausing)	(wait for it)
(NOW!)	
dash	

    more flash

        add brash

            then B-A-S-H!

final pose
CUT!
THAT'S A WRAP!

Do Views Rule?

> **JUST KITTEN AROUND Joke**
>
> Q: What did the elevator operator say when the kitten asked him how to spell "Mississippi?"
>
> A: "The river or the state?"

During lunch, PittyPat strolled into the cafeteria. As a water cat, her wet fur was groomed daily, so she was all gold and glam. Angel sat with Jazz, as usual, but gladly made room for her sister. They all gossiped while they ate fish sticks.

Finally PittyPat said, "Angel, let's take a walk together."

"Why?" Angel asked.

"We need to talk," PittyPat said.

"Sure." Angel wondered if something was wrong. "I've got time."

They only waited a few minutes at the elevator.

"Ninth floor. Cafeteria. Going down."

PittyPat stepped into the elevator, followed by Angel.

"Afternoon, Miss Persian. Miss Persian," Mr. Sean said.

PittyPat and Angel rolled their eyes and bumped shoulders as if to say, "Miss Persian" was a strange way to address them.

"First floor. The Director's office and Majestic Kennels Visitors' Center. Going up."

When she exited, Angel automatically turned toward the west wing. She couldn't be this close to the leaderboard and not check it. Her coyote video with the horrible blue cape had gone down one spot to number twelve. Angel was relieved it hadn't fallen farther. But number twelve was terrible.

PittyPat's latest water video was number seven. With a start, Angel realized that she hadn't seen PittyPat's latest video. She always watched Quincy's and PittyPat's videos and anything from DaddyAlbert. This week, though, she'd been so busy—with what? Worrying about her own videos and the leaderboard, she thought guiltily.

PittyPat barely looked at the leaderboard, and a few minutes later they strolled down the street, side by side. Kittywood was blooming, the gardeners creating a summertime show of color and smells.

Along the sidewalk, Angel lifted her nose to smell a lovely pink rose.

"I'm worried about you," PittyPat said.

Turning, Angel said, "About what?"

"You're stuck on the leaderboard. How many times did you come down this morning to check it?"

Angel said nothing, her stomach twisting.

"How many?" PittyPat asked again.

"Only a couple times," Angel said.

"Mr. Sean said you rode the elevator four times this morning," PittyPat said. "And eight times yesterday. You go down every hour to check."

"So what?" Angel's face flushed with embarrassment. She walked faster to get in front of PittyPat. She stopped abruptly and spun to face her sister. "So what? Who cares how many times I check the leaderboard?"

PittyPat's green eyes widened, and she stared at Angel.

Angel spun away. "Who cares?"

"You care. And you care too much," PittyPat said.

Angel's head ached. Yes, she cared too much. She needed to be in the top twenty kittens. And she needed to get another number one video. And another. And another. Of course she cared.

"You're not happy," PittyPat said. "You need to enjoy your work. Don't let the leaderboards destroy you, or you won't last."

Angel tried to turn the conversation to PittyPat. "Do you enjoy your baths? All that water?"

PittyPat just shrugged and strolled on. "Of course I do. Do you enjoy being the Underdog Cat?"

Angel thought about the Underdog Cat role. At first it had been fun. No one expected her to do anything as an underdog. It was like they were daring her to do something wild and crazy. That kind of challenge filled her with glee, like doing a double flip in acrobatics last night. She enjoyed proving that she could do something difficult.

But Underdog Cat always saved the day. Always. It was expected. She had to win because Underdog Cat would never lose, and that made her role, well, boring. The outcome was never in question.

Underdog Cat didn't have weaknesses. No kryptonite.

"It's been a good role for me," Angel said. "I'm just tired of it. Maybe I should find another role. But what?"

"It's not only that." PittyPat locked eyes with her and Angel couldn't look away. "It's deeper. You care about the leaderboard."

Angel wanted to run away from this conversation. But PittyPat had always been able to cut through everything and make her think. Angel forced herself to understand what the leaderboards meant. Yes, she did care about the scores, about who was on top. Maybe it was her family; growing up as the child of Grace and Albert Persian was hard. The records they held for views had never been broken. Angel slowed her walk and stepped off the sidewalk into the Catnip Meadow. Rubbing her face in the catnip distracted her.

"Maybe it's MamaGrace and DaddyAlbert," she said.

"You're still a kitten," PittyPat said. "You have many years to beat their records."

"Oh, no. No one can match them," Angel said.

"That's not true," PittyPat said. "Give yourself, and the rest of us, a chance to grow up. We'll find our own records."

"You're so reasonable," Angel said. "So easygoing."

"I have ambition too," PittyPat said. "But I'm not letting it kill my joy."

Angel knew PittyPat was right. Something had to change so she loved her videos again. And she had to start ignoring the leaderboards. But even now, she needed to dash back to Majestic Kennels

Survivors

MamaGrace sat beside Captain Piper, looking out at the skyline of Kittywood. Yesterday Angel had talked and talked about the acrobatics class. So, MamaGrace had invited the captain to her penthouse apartment to talk.

"We're alike, you know," MamaGrace said.

"No. You're a Persian cat, and I'm a woman and an ex-marine."

"We're both victims."

Captain Piper's hand crept up to trace the scar on her cheek. She dropped her hand. "I've moved on."

"Yes. Of course," MamaGrace said. "You're tough, and you'll be fine. But it doesn't change the facts. We're both victims."

"The driver who hit you—how did it happen?" Captain Piper asked.

MamaGrace patted her eye patch. "They told me he was texting his wife. He was telling her that he was on his way to pick up Grace Persian—me!

She was a big fan of my videos. He wanted to get a picture with me to send to her."

Drivers licensed in Kittywood knew to look down toward the ground for cats and kittens. But he'd been too busy texting to see MamaGrace. She'd been run over by the front wheel and had barely survived.

Captain Piper nodded. "My buddy was a mechanic who repaired military tanks. One day, he actually got to drive a tank. He was so excited, he was taking selfies and sending them to his girlfriend. That's when he hit me."

MamaGrace laid a paw on Captain Piper's leg. Gently, softly, she said, "And yet, here we are! You and me, Captain, we're survivors."

Captain Piper's lips tightened in a straight line. Deliberately, she smiled and repeated, "Survivors."

What They Call Me

WHAT MAMA GRACE CALLS ME

She calls me chameleon
because I long for the number one video,
while staying invisible.

I wish I were graceful,
comfortable with fame—
like her.

WHAT JAZZ CALLS ME

She calls me a blind rat
because I can't see
my own career:
I'm visionless.

I wish I were confident,
waving to fans, amid cheers—
like her.

WHAT RUDY CALLS ME

He calls me a peacock
because I am groomed
every day—I shine,

inside and out.

I wish I could go
one day unkempt—
like him.

EPISODE 4
Piano Cat

L IGHTS!
  CAMERA!
  ACTION!

A C T   1 :

A tiny black-and-white kitten leaps onto a piano. He leans forward and uses his delicate paw to strike a note.

Aaah! sings the piano.

The kitten leans his head to the right and strikes the piano again.

Aaah! sings the piano.

The kitten leans his head to the left and strikes the piano again.

Aaah! sings the piano.

Aaah! sings the kitten.

A C T   2 :

The kitten looks at himself in the mirror above the keys. He kneads his claws on the keys in excitement. At the bass end of the keyboard, the kitten springs. Clang!

But then he delicately walks on black keys only, from the bass to the alto to the soprano notes, singing as he walks. The camera focuses on his tidy paws, spreading with his weight and contracting as he lifted it for the next step.

Aaah! sings the piano. *Aaah!* sings the kitten, matching the piano's note each time.

The kitten turns and walks back on white keys only, from soprano to alto to bass.

Aaah! sings the piano. *Aaah!* sings the kitten, matching the piano's note each time.

At the end, the kitten sprawls on the keys and looks around.

Aaah! sings the kitten.

And the piano answers, *Aaah!*

CUT.

THAT'S A WRAP!

(Note to film editor: Apply a black and white noir filter to this episode.)

The Angel Costume

The taxi halted in front of the warehouse, and the driver hopped out to open the door. Angel peered up at a redbrick-and-steel building; it was imposing. Did she really want to do this?

She stepped out of the elevator into the loft studio, large windows on each wall. *This would be a cheerful place to work*, she thought.

Miss Emily stood before a form of a cat, pinning a costume onto it. She nodded at Angel but kept working.

Curious, Angel walked around the costume, trying to see it from different angles. "What is it?"

"I'm working on ideas for holidays. I'm just working ahead." She gestured to a line of drawings taped on the wall. Halloween masks for October. Candy stripe for December.

Angel studied the designs and realized that everything was adapted for Jazz's costumes. It was smart to be working ahead like this.

Miss Emily put one last pin into the cat form and turned to Angel. "What can I do for you today?"

Angel didn't want this conversation, but it had to be done. "You heard about the blue cape?"

Miss Emily pressed her lips together but said nothing.

"The Director says that next time, I have to do a test video."

Miss Emily raised an eyebrow. "Next time?"

"Yes," Angel said. "I'd like to try an angel costume."

"Oh." Miss Emily tilted her head, studying Angel. "Why?"

"I messed up with the blue cape. I should've let the Director do a test video. But that doesn't mean I've given up on the idea of a costume. The Director named me Angel. People like to see angels, right? I just think, maybe, who knows, but maybe…"

Miss Emily motioned for Angel to stay still and then strolled around her. She grabbed a notebook and feverishly drew. "We don't need much. Let her own fur shine through," she mumbled as if Angel were no longer there. "Basically, we just need a halo and wings." She hooked a leg around a table, leaning over her work and pulling pens and watercolor brushes close.

Angel leaped onto the table to pace in front of the paper, watching the images take shape. There was a white fluffy Persian—did she look like that?

With quick, sure strokes, Miss Emily added a halo and large, majestic wings, and then started adding details.

Within a few minutes, Miss Emily stopped to turn the page around for Angel's inspection. "What do you think?"

Angel blinked in surprise. The costume was much simpler than Jazz's costumes, which was good. "For the 'Underdog Cat vs. Coyote' video," Angel said, "I had to run along a path through the woods. Those wings would be in the way."

Miss Emily let her left hand stroke her chin while she stared out toward the docks. Her right hand hovered over the paper. "Collapsible wings? No. That's silly. Well, does she really need wings? Or just a halo?"

She flipped to a new page, bent over the paper, and drew again. Finally she flipped the page up for Angel.

The drawing showed a Persian cat with a golden halo and small, feathered wings that hugged close to the body. These weren't the majestic wings of the first drawing; instead they were whimsical, yet useful.

"When you run through an obstacle course, you'll be able to fold them up."

Angel shook her head. "That sounds hard. How much time would it take?"

Miss Emily grimaced. "Oh. Time. Well, you could stop the action, fold them down, and then go on. But the Director won't like that. He always wants to film straight through. Do you know what action you'll be doing?"

"I'm Underdog Cat," Angel said. "I have to perform heroic deeds. Except this time, I'll also be angelic."

"So, you'll be in action. Okay, let me try again."

Rolling her head in a circle, Miss Emily raised her shoulders and let them drop heavily. She rose and walked to the wall of shelves. She wore leggings and a loose shirt so she could easily stretch up and touch boxes. Her hand passed lightly across the row of boxes, pausing now and then as if to remind herself what was inside.

Abruptly she strode back to the table and hunched over the drawing pad, making bold, thick lines. Shaking her head, she ripped off the sheet and started on a fresh one.

I'm not needed here, Angel thought. *Just let her work.*

She wandered to the window and leaned against the warm glass, watching the docks below. But the sunshine made her sleepy. She glanced back at Miss

Emily, who tore off yet another sheet of paper and furiously scribbled on the next page. Angel curled up in the sun and took a nap.

Studio 9

Every year I say I quit.
Had my fill of viral videos.
Had my fill of goblin cats,
chonk cats,
and "Yeah, that's a cat!" cats.

Had enough of KittyTube—
of the Director yelling,
the pressure for new ideas,
the rat race to reach number one.
Growl!
We're supposed to eat rats,
not chase them.

And then there's the movie.
Filming *Puss and Boots* in France
For LeChat Carré studio—
That was exciting.
The premiere was exciting.
The movie going worldwide is exciting.

It's all so...exciting,
in an exciting sort of way.
You know what I mean?

But being back here at Majestic Kennels—
a cat can sure catch
a lot of snoozes—*zzz!*—
in sunny spots.
Or laugh with other KittyTubers
about the silliness
that entertains humans.
Or snuggle up with my Grace,
my sweet Grace,
the love of my life, Grace.

KittyTube, meow!
Unless I get another movie script,
Well...meow,
I need to work.

Look out, Studio 9.
Albert Persian is coming!

EPISODE 5

The Ivory Bongo Harp Band

> ## JUST KITTEN AROUND Joke
> Q: What did the alien say to the Ivory Bongo Harp Band?
> A: I've traveled across the galaxy to meet you! On my home planet, we love KittyTube.

The screen is dark, with glorious music playing.

A spotlight stabs the dark. Rudy, the black-and-white piano cat, is racing up and down the black and white keys. His tiny paws tickle the ivory keyboard.

Another spotlight stabs the dark. Maria, another tiny Devon, stands beside a golden harp. She unsheathes her claws. Carefully, gently, she plucks a string. Her paws move across the harp's strings, bringing forth an angelic melody.

Another spotlight stabs the dark. Curly, a Singapura kitten, thumps on a bongo, holding the piano and harp music together with a steady beat. Singapura cats are itty-bitty (the smallest breed of cats), but Curly pounds the bongo with HUGE sweeps of her paws, creating a HUGE thump, Thump, THUMP. While she keeps the beat, Curly also sings, her meows weaving in and out of the piano and harp melodies.

It's a band of three tiny kittens.

But they create a mighty and glorious sound.

Meet the Ivory Bongo Harp Band.

The newest and hottest sensation on KittyTube.

EPISODE 6
Testing The Angel Costume

Miss Tanya looked Angel over one last time, her comb hovering. She nodded. "Perfect. The angel costume is lovely."

Miss Tanya never commented on how Angel looked, so her words were encouraging. Narrow wings hovered over her shoulders, and a classic gold ring crowned her head. Its simplicity made it stunning. Anything more complicated would have looked fussy.

Angel walked onto the stage.

A camera operator whistled and called, "Wow!"

Angel's heart lifted. This would be a viral video! Given her name, the angel costume had always been inevitable. The Director would love this. After all, MamaGrace said that the Director had given her the name of Angel.

Lights flared on, and Angel's heart flared with hope. For this test video, Angel had to run through a simple obstacle course: a chair, a box, a bowl of water. She was supposed to run as close as possible to each object.

The Director called, "Action."

Angel looked at the camera a long time for her odd-eyed soul-connect. "Watch me, watch me, watch me," she told the video camera. "I'm angelic."

She turned and sprinted. The chair was metal, a collapsible, foldable one. She dashed to its right, but at the last second—it was too tempting—she sent her hind legs first and slid under the chair. Leaping up, she flashed the camera a wicked smile.

The cardboard box reminded Angel of the foam cubes in the acrobatics class. She leaped onto the box and charged off the other side, legs and tail spread wide. *I'm a lightning bolt,* she thought.

She ran toward the bowl of water, intending to slide around it. She went in feet-first again, but this time she careened out of control into the water bowl, which flipped over. She was drenched.

Oh, Angel thought. *That wasn't very angelic.*

The set was silent.

Finally, from beyond the lights, came the Director's voice. "Cut!"

The Director stepped onto the stage, his front legs stiff, chest puffed out. Glaring, he shook a paw at her. "What was that?"

Angel backed away, putting a water puddle between them. Because he was hairless, the Director hated getting wet and cold. The water would protect her. She hoped.

He glared and repeated, "What was that?"

Angel looked aside. "You said to run the obstacle course, so I did."

"Your angel costume is ruined. You left the halo at the box."

Reaching up a paw to her head, Angel spun around. On the ground near the cube, she saw the halo. It must have fallen off when she jumped off as if struck by lightning.

"Oh, my wings…" She tried to look around at them.

"Wet feathers. Ruined." The Director almost spat the words.

Angel shrank to her belly, pulling her paws over her head to brush away some water.

The studio was utterly silent.

"The obstacle course…"

"No!" roared the Director. "Just say you're sorry."

Angel sucked in a deep breath, meaning to explain everything. Instead, she squeaked, "Sorry."

The Director stomped through the water puddle and stood over her. "Angel Persian, you don't need to wear costumes. I don't care how adorable they are. You're not a costume person. Don't try another one."

Angel peered up at him.

The Director shivered, his skin covered with goose bumps.

"But..." Angel tried.

"No."

"Maybe..." Angel tried again.

"No."

"Why?" Her voice broke with frustration.

"No. You are Underdog Cat. Jazz wears costumes. You do NOT! Now go get cleaned up. We'll do an episode in thirty minutes. Without the costume."

Angel trembled now, emotions swirling. She just needed to get the top video again, and costumes worked for Jazz. Why not for her? How else could she get the top video more than once?

This was so unfair. The costumes were a shortcut, a gimmick, a trick to make her videos more interesting. She needed the viewers to click and click and click.

Angel rose and wobbled to the dressing room. She expected Miss Tanya to be mad, to tell her what a fool she'd been. Instead, the petite woman just pulled out the hair dryer. Making herself small, Angel hunched her shoulders against the heat.

The door pushed open, and Rudy peered around. "Are you okay?"

"No," Angel said. "No costumes for me."

Rudy shrugged. "You don't need costumes. Your white fur is your costume."

Angel shook water from one paw, making Miss Tanya step back.

The groomer frowned at Angel, who rolled her eyes and said, "Sorry. I didn't mean to do that."

Rudy said, "I wonder..." But he stopped, shaking his head.

"What?"

Rudy stepped backward to allow Miss Tanya to walk around Angel. "I shouldn't say anything."

"What?" Angel was curious now.

"Well, what if you did an acrobatics video?"

Angel turned to Rudy, waving off Miss Tanya for a moment. "We aren't ready for that yet."

Rudy shrugged.

"I can only do a single flip. Nothing else."

Rudy shrugged.

"The Director will get mad."

"Not if the video gets views," Rudy said. "What do you have to lose?"

"No. I won't do it without talking to the Director first."

"Okay." Rudy shrugged. "Talk to him."

Angel squared her shoulders and shot her tail toward the sky. "Yes. I'll do that right now." She marched out the door.

On a Roll

HAHAHA

JUST KITTEN AROUND Joke

Girl 1: What do cats say when they get hurt?

Girl 2: Tell me.

Girl 1: Me-OW!

A lanky man stood before a black screen. He wore dark clothing and sunglasses. Obviously, he wasn't the star of this video. That was the fluffy white cat perched on his shoulder.

Angel tried hard to keep her claws sheathed so she wouldn't hurt Mr. Leon. He held up a white ring. Angel took a sharp breath and leaped through the ring, thinking about the excitement. If the viewer could just feel the thrill of this leap...

This is astounding, she thought.

She flipped over once before instinctively landing on the ground on her feet.

When she looked up, the Director was grimacing. "Not very exciting," he said. "Try it again."

Frowning, she let Mr. Leon pick her up and put her on his shoulder.

Angel didn't like it when Mr. Leon picked her up. He wanted to pet her, but he used some kind of sticky lotion, and it clumped her fur.

"Wait," Angel said. "Miss Tanya, I need you."

Miss Tanya brushed Angel's fur until every hair was in place again.

Angel thought that if Miss Tanya had to come in again, she'd insist that Mr. Leon use a leather shoulder pad. Her every muscle was taut, trying to stay upright without digging her claws into him.

The Director repositioned the camera operators, with one focusing on shoulder height and another lying on the floor so she could shoot a close-up at the end of the trick.

The Director called, "Get ready."

"Quiet on the set!"

"Action!"

Mr. Leon glanced at her, but Angel kept her eyes on the camera at shoulder height. As soon as she jumped, she'd look down at the other camera. They'd use the two angles and cut them together for the video.

Angel used her odd-colored eyes for a soul-connect with the audience. When Mr. Leon held up the white ring, she vaulted. She thought about the thrill of doing leaps, twirls, and somersaults. In her head, she saw a crowd cheering in excitement. There was, well, excitement. Before she was ready, she landed on the floor beside the camera operator.

Another clean flip! If only she could do a double.

She ambled, tail high, toward the camera for another soul-connect. She ended with a quiet "Meow. Eh!"

The set was silent.

The camera operator yawned.

Angel glared, bewildered.

The camera operator waved a hand. "Oh, sorry. I didn't get enough sleep last night."

Was he bored with her performance?

"Yowza! Did you get enough sleep last night, Angel?" the Director said. "You're off today."

Double Flip

HAHAHA

> ## JUST KITTEN AROUND Joke
> Q: What do you call a pile of kittens?
> A: A meow-ntain!

The Blue Room was half lit by the hallway light, and that was enough for Angel. She didn't need to draw attention to herself. She didn't want anyone to know she was here again, practicing.

Captain Piper had left the staircase of cubes set up.

Angel climbed to the second cube and stood at the edge, looking down. The camera operator and the Director didn't like the acrobatics video. They had posted it last night, along with every other kitten's video, because she had to have a video every week. But she didn't expect it to do well.

So why was she here? Why was she trying to perform even harder tricks like the double flip?

Angel ground her teeth. She was here because this was something she liked, something she needed to do for herself. Her stomach fluttered in excitement.

"Jump!" she yelled.

She leaped, tucking her head and doing a perfect single flip, landing lightly on her feet.

It felt right. It felt natural.

She trotted back to the staircase and climbed to the third cube. From this height, a double flip was possible. She was determined to get it right.

Deep breath. Angel leaped, tucking her head, spinning once, and again. Except, coming out of the second spin too early—oh, no, no—she had to twist, get her feet under her body.

Quick!

Somehow, she landed on her feet. Barely.

She exhaled. That was close. She needed to get it right!

Think. What did she do right? Wrong?

For one thing, she needed to speed up. The height of four cubes might give her enough time to spin around twice. She raced up the cubes to the top.

This time she didn't wait or think about the jump. She just walked to the edge, leaped, tucked, spun, and spun.

And landed. A perfect double flip.

She'd done it! Like it was nothing. Easy. Natural.

It couldn't be that easy. She had to do it again.

Quickly she ran to the stairs and climbed up to the fourth cube.

Don't wait, she told herself. *Don't overthink this.*

She leaped—

"Angel!" called Rudy.

She tucked—

"There you are!" called Jazz.

Distracted, she spun wildly, wobbling—

"Angel!" called PittyPat.

She fell out of control, flipping somehow to land on her feet. Ow! Her front leg crumpled.

Looking up, she saw her friends and her sister staring at her with wide eyes.

"What were you doing?" PittyPat yelled.

Rudy shook his head. "Are you trying a double without Captain Piper here to spot you?"

Jazz knelt beside her. "What's wrong?"

Angel blinked, pain shooting up her leg.

Jazz took over. "Rudy, get Mr. Sean to phone down for a doctor. PittyPat, get over here and help me."

Rudy shot out the door while PittyPat kept Angel from sitting up.

"Wait for the doctor," PittyPat said, and Jazz agreed.

Rudy reappeared a few minutes later, Mr. Sean behind him. Mr. Sean wanted to pick her up and carry her downstairs.

But Jazz forbade it. "Don't move her until the doctor arrives."

While they waited, Angel said, "Why are you all here, anyway?"

"Oh," Jazz said. "We forgot."

PittyPat's face lit up. "We've been trying to find you. It's your acrobatics video—"

"The one the Director didn't like," interrupted Rudy.

"The one that put the camera operator to sleep?" Angel said. She blinked, trying not to cry at the memory.

Bouncing on his toes, Rudy said, "You'll never guess—"

"It's hit number one," Jazz said. "You did it!"

"And not only that," PittyPat said, "but it's shooting high enough to rank on the overall chart with the adult cats at number twenty. None of the kittens has ever done that before."

Puzzled, Angel realized that she hadn't been down to look at the leaderboard today. In fact, she'd never even thought about it. She'd been so wrapped up in trying to perfect her double flip that the leaderboard...well, it just didn't matter. She said dumbly, "Acrobatics. Number one?"

Her friends cried, "Yes!"

"That can't be," Angel said. "It was so much fun to do."

"And that," Jazz said, "is why you hit number one. You've finally found something you love to do." She frowned at Angel's leg. "I just hope it doesn't kill you!"

From Twenty-seven
to Twenty

Angel, Quincy, PittyPat, and Jazz nestled in some pillows conveniently set near the stage and waited.

Angel had limped into the meeting room, careful to walk on three legs. Her front leg was sprained but not broken. She just had to take it easy for a week or two. She'd still do a video this week, but a quiet one. Snuggling with friends was a pleasant way to rest her leg.

Maria and Curly lay on a nearby pillow with Rudy. Their Ivory Bongo Harp Band had the number two kitten video for the week. Angel was glad to see Rudy finding his place on KittyTube. Music was a sweet spot for him.

Other kittens slouched all around.

Today was the day. The kittens would go from twenty-seven to only twenty.

Three of the kittens had already said they were moving on to other jobs at the kennels. TyAdam would work with lights, Rhapsody in the editing room, and Isobelle with advertising. Two more had decided to work in their family's businesses of shipping and retail stores.

That still left two more kittens who would be cut today and have to find other jobs.

Angel wondered what she'd do if they cut her. She wouldn't be cut this time, but next time, when only ten kittens were left, it could happen. What else would she do?

Choreography, she thought. I'd help cats plan how they move across a stage.

There were many jobs besides acting. Important jobs.

The Director arrived and stomped to the stage. "I want to inspire you," he said. "You need to be inspired."

But his voice was rough, his skin was wrinkled, and he looked old.

"Okay, here's the cut. TyAdam, Rhapsody, Isobelle, Berta, Mirko, CC. and Hugo. You're cut."

Just like that, the world changed for the seven kittens.

Quincy whispered, "C.C. has been offered a job taste-testing for the new restaurant chain that's coming in, the Gledhill Fish Company."

Angel nodded. Berta and Mirko would go to their family businesses. That just left Hugo who'd need to find a job. He'd done some videos with PittyPat, but it hadn't helped him find an audience. Since he was their cousin, she was sure DaddyAlbert and MamaGrace would help. Hugo would be fine.

"The rest of you?" the Director said. "You're all on a roll. You'll all move on. But in another month, we'll cut to the top ten. There are too many adult cat actors already. You must build your audience, or the kennels won't offer you a contract for the next year. The question is this: Which kitten to watch?"

Later, the friends gathered in Jazz and Angel's dorm room to talk.

"What will the future hold for us?" Quincy said.

"Any way it goes, it's okay," Angel said. "I could be a choreographer and be happy. Or a stunt cat. Or a star."

Rudy said, "You really helped me find my piano cat role, which led to the band. Music works well for me. You could also be a casting director. Or develop ideas for videos."

Angel nodded. "I could."

Jazz said, "You like change. Maybe you'll do all of that at some time. Me? I love the dress-up cat role. I could do this forever—if my views stay high. If my audience develops."

Quincy said, "I love food."

Angel punched his stomach with her paw. "You love it too much. Be careful, or you'll only get to do fat-cat roles."

PittyPat said, "I don't know. I like the water cat role. But I'll look around at other ideas too. It's so hard to look good when you're slicked down with water."

"Oh, you'll grow up to be a golden cat, like DaddyAlbert. Make everything in your video a gold metal, scatter gold glitter in the air…"

"There she goes," Rudy said, "planning your next role for you. Personally, I'd let her do it."

Made in United States
Orlando, FL
06 January 2022